Éric Faye
Born in Limoges, Éric Faye is a journalist and the prize-winning author of more than twenty books.

Emily Boyce
Emily Boyce is in-house translator at Gallic Books. She lives in London.

Nagasaki

Nagasaki

Éric Faye

Translated from the French by Emily Boyce

Gallic Books

London

A Gallic Book

First published in France as *Nagasaki* by Éditions Stock 2012
Copyright © Éditions Stock 2012

English translation copyright © Gallic Books 2014
First published in Great Britain in 2014
by Gallic Books, 59 Ebury Street,
London, SW1W 0NZ

A CIP record for this book is available from the British Library
ISBN 978-1-908313-65-2

Typeset in Fournier MT & Georgia by Gallic Books
Printed in the UK by CPI Group (UK) Ltd, Croydon, CR0 4YY
2 4 6 8 10 9 7 5 3 1

It is said that all bamboos of the same stock
flower together and die together,
no matter how far apart they are planted.

Pascal Quignard

This novel is based on a story which appeared in several Japanese newspapers, including *Asahi*, in May 2008.

Imagine a man in his fifties disappointed to have reached middle age so quickly and utterly, residing in his modest house in a suburb of Nagasaki with very steep streets. Picture these snakes of soft asphalt slithering up the hillsides until they reach the point where all the urban scum of corrugated iron, tarpaulins, tiles and God knows what else peters out beside a wall of straggly, crooked bamboo. That is where I live. Who am I? Without wishing to overstate matters, I don't amount to much. As a single man, I cultivate certain habits which keep me out of trouble and allow me to tell myself I have at least some redeeming features.

One of these habits is avoiding as far as possible going out for a drink with my colleagues after work. I like to have time to myself at home before eating dinner at a reasonable hour: never later than 6.30 p.m. If I were married, I don't suppose I would stick to such a rigid routine, and would probably go out with them more often, but I'm not (married, that is). I'm fifty-six, by the way.

That day, I was feeling a little under the weather, so I came home earlier than usual. It must have been before five when the tram dropped me in my road with a shopping bag over each arm. I rarely get back so early during the week, and as I went inside I felt almost as if I was trespassing. That's putting it a bit strongly, and yet … Until quite recently, I hardly ever locked the door when I went out; ours is a safe area and several of my old-lady neighbours (Mrs Ota, Mrs Abe and some others a bit further away) are at home most of the time. On days when I have a lot to carry, it's handy if the door is unlocked: all I have to do is get off the tram, walk a few steps, pull the sliding door across, and I'm inside. I just take off my shoes, put on my slippers and I'm ready to put the shopping away. Afterwards, I usually sit down and draw breath, but I didn't have that luxury this time: at the sight of the fridge, the previous day's concerns came flooding back to me all at once.

When I opened it, however, nothing seemed out of the ordinary. Everything was in the right place, which is to say the place I had left it that morning. The pickled vegetables, cubes of tofu, the eels set aside for dinner. I carefully inspected each glass shelf. Soy sauce and radishes, dried kelp and red-bean paste, raw octopus in a Tupperware container. On the bottom shelf, all four triangular pouches of seaweed rice were present and correct. The two aubergines were there as well. I felt a weight lifting from me, especially since I was convinced the ruler would provide extra assurance. It's a stainless-steel one, forty centimetres long. I stuck a strip of blank paper to the unmarked side and plunged it into a carton of fruit juice (with added vitamins A, C and E) that I had opened that morning. I waited a few seconds, just long enough for my probe to soak up the liquid, and then I slowly pulled it out. I hardly dared look. Eight centimetres, I read. Only eight centimetres of juice remained, compared to fifteen when I had left for work. Someone had been helping themselves to it. And yet I live alone.

My fears boiled up again. To make absolutely sure, I checked the notebook where I had been recording levels and quantities for several days. Yes, it had definitely been fifteen that morning. Once I had even gone as far as taking a photograph of the inside of the fridge, but had never done it since. Either I couldn't be bothered or had felt stupid. That was in the days before I knew for sure; any remaining doubts had now vanished. I had new evidence that something really was going on, the third such sign in the last fortnight, and bear in mind I'm a very rational person, not someone who would believe a ghost was popping in to quench his thirst and polish off the leftovers.

My suspicions had first been aroused several weeks earlier, but had rapidly disappeared. Yet some time later they came back in a vague sort of way, rather like midges that buzz around in the evening air and then fly off before you've quite registered they're there. The whole thing began one day when I was certain I had bought some food that I then couldn't find. My instinctive reaction was, naturally, to doubt myself. It's so easy to convince yourself you put something in your shopping trolley when in fact you only meant to. It's so tempting to put memory lapses down to tiredness. Tiredness is used as an excuse for almost anything!

The second time, by chance, I had kept the till receipt and was able to confirm I had not imagined it: I really had bought the fish that had since vanished into thin air. This didn't make things any clearer though; I remained mystified and no closer to an explanation. I was rattled. The inside of my fridge was, in a sense, the ever-changing source of my future: the molecules that would provide me with energy in the coming days were contained within it in the form of aubergines, mango juice and whatever else. Tomorrow's microbes, toxins and proteins awaited me in that cold antechamber, and the thought of a stranger's hand taking from it at random and putting my future self in jeopardy shook me to the core. Worse: it repulsed me. It was nothing short of a kind of violation.

The night did nothing to dispel my unease over the disappearing fruit juice. In the morning, I set my nit-picking mind to piecing together the puzzle. At times like this the brain investigates, reconstructs, corroborates, deduces, unpicks, juxtaposes, supposes, calculates, suspects. I ended up cursing that grey Sanyo fridge with the slogan 'Always with you' slyly printed across it. Was there such a thing as a haunted refrigerator? Or one that fed itself by skimming off part of its contents? When I got back from work, I was eager to do something to calm my anxiety, which was slowly becoming a form of torture. At just gone six o'clock, there was still time … It was a last resort and I would probably feel ridiculous doing it, but my stress levels were now such that I simply had to know. To hell with the routine, I would eat dinner late.

I put my coat and shoes back on, went out, and caught a tram heading down towards Hamanomachi. The shop where I intended to purchase my new 'trap' was only two stops away and, providing my DIY skills were up to the task, I would sleep more peacefully afterwards.

In fact I didn't need to put my handyman credentials to the test, as the device turned out to be much easier to fit than I had anticipated. I would have to wait until I was at work the next day to put my plan into action, a strategy that would make my fridge readings look like Stone Age techniques. I would aim to get in as early as possible and be at my desk by 8 a.m. I was relieved to be taking action but impatient to get started and, to tell the truth, beginning to lose the plot: it was after nine when I realised I hadn't had a bite to eat. Oh well, just this once.

Sitting in my armchair with a pot of hot tea beside me, I tried to take my mind off things by watching TV, but nothing gripped my attention. Instead I picked up the magazine I subscribe to but never normally read. On page 37, a picture of a horribly wrinkled man caught my eye. 'Tanabe Tomoji hasn't touched a drop of alcohol in his life,' declared the journalist. As I skimmed the article, I couldn't help thinking what a fool this man was. Tanabe, the oldest man alive, maintained he had got to the age of 113 eating nothing but vegetables and the occasional deep-fried prawn as a treat. Well, he sounded like a real live wire. This living fossil's last remaining source of pleasure consisted of peeling a prawn or two, though he was eating fewer and fewer of them because greasy foods no longer agreed with him. Poor old Tanabe! Soon you'll be welcomed into nirvana and everything will be all right, you'll see: they've put a fried-prawn stand right by the entrance and you can stuff yourself to your heart's content without worrying about the oil.

It seems ridiculous now, but at the time I was captivated; I stopped thinking about my trap and read the article from beginning to end. 'I'm happy,' the old fogey told them. 'I want to live another ten years.' Silly twerp! And I don't know why but afterwards, oblivious to the sun going down amid the far-off rumble of traffic, I stayed for some time sitting in the dark, looking out of the bay window but not seeing the bay itself, the looming ships or the dockyard.

At that point in the evening you assume that your waking self with all its sediment of bitterness, worries, regrets or remorse and jealousy, will dissolve in a deep sleep, until the night veers off course. Though no different from usual – no louder, no quieter – the cicadas wake you the second you start drifting off. They screech on and on, driving you to distraction like drunken harpies; or are you being over-sensitive tonight? Here they come, single file into your head through one ear and out the other, circling around your skull before diving in again, spiralling malevolently in their line, laughing mockingly. Mercifully a violent downpour disperses them before dawn like the protesters on the NHK news last night, driven from wherever it was by water cannons. But how can you doze off knowing that with a simple copy of the key, the intruder – since there obviously is one – can let themselves into your home at any moment, together with a gang of heavies to beat you up and leave you for dead before you even know what's happening to you? You think to yourself: it's because of you, intruder, that I can't sleep, and I'll have a terrible headache later sitting in front of my areas of high and low pressure, but just you wait. You'll get what's coming to you. Everything is in place. And look, it's time to get up; it's already six thirty.

There comes a time when nothing happens any more. The ribbon of destiny, stretched too wide, has snapped. There's no more. The shockwave caused by your birth is far, oh so far, behind you now. That is modern life. Your existence spans the distance between failure and success. Between frost and the rising of sap. I had been mulling all this over on the tram the previous week, and that morning, as I sat in the same spot on the tram, looking out at the same urban wallpaper, the thought that it might not be set in stone made me euphoric. The vehicle hurtled along, taking in the stops, taking in pensive, silent humans preoccupied with trying to decipher unfathomable dreams. Maybe they lived more fully in their sleep than in their waking hours? After a litany of stations I knew by heart – Kankodori, Edomachi and Ohato, Gotomachi followed by Yachiyomachi then Takaramachi – I got off and changed onto another line. Sometimes I finish my journey on foot, but this morning I wasn't up to it, and besides I was in a hurry. No sooner had I left the metallic grating sound of the tram behind me than the cicadas took over, screeching as I walked under their trees. They were judging me, confounding my thoughts and barely formed sentences so that as soon as I reached the office I shut the windows and asked my colleagues to give me a moment: I was up all night because of them and they're hysterical this morning, listen to them; it makes you want to block your ears, and even then, when everything's sealed up, they still find a way in; they can get through glass and concrete, they pass through walls, these creatures – which brought my mind back to the matter in hand: the camera, and my very own person who walks through walls.

I retreated to my desk, alone. As far as my colleagues knew, I was busy studying the overnight satellite photos; because, like them, I am a meteorologist. Once I've logged on to my computer and launched the relevant programs, I spend each morning consulting the latest charts and reports sent in from various weather stations. Since on this occasion there was no need to issue any weather warnings or attend to any other urgent tasks, I opened a window in the bottom right-hand corner of my screen. In the space of a few clicks, I had set the trap. It was done. As if by magic, a still shot of a kitchen appeared, the same kitchen where I had just been eating my breakfast. Everything looked calm. If I had been married with a wife at home, I could have watched her moving about from my desk. Before leaving the office of an evening, I would know what she was making for dinner. The webcam I had installed the previous day worked brilliantly. Without leaving my seat, I could be an invisible, weightless ninja spying on my own home. I had achieved ubiquity without even trying. But then the telephone rang, telling me I was needed. The departmental meeting scheduled for ten o'clock had been brought forward and was starting any minute. Blast, just as I was trying to concentrate on the little aquarium in the bottom right-hand corner of my screen.

Later on, once the meeting had finished, I resumed my watch, regaining the use of my third eye. It's possible to link these tiny webcams to your mobile phone, which is exactly what I should have done had mine not been prehistoric (three years old). Then I wouldn't have had to waste my time during the meeting; I could have carried on watching the house while listening to them listening to each other, repeating each other, rehashing each other. If I was married, I could keep an eye on my wife, either out of jealousy or because I couldn't bear to be parted from her. Passing in front of the camera, she would wink flirtatiously at my third eye, perhaps even blow it a kiss. Come the afternoon, I would know which friends she had round and what they were wearing. But today, the camera was far from being a chastity belt or any other marital tie. From inside the glass cabinet where I had installed it, the camera unveiled a chilling picture of my solitude which made me shiver if I dwelt on it. Luckily I had no time to dwell on it because the telephone rang, a colleague asking my advice, and I fine-tuned the shipping forecast: my job consists of pre-emptively saving the lives of fishermen from Tsushima-to to Tanega-shima and beyond.

As the morning wore on, so the cicadas kept up their racket. I was at their mercy, my nerves in tatters. They could force a confession from any suspect.

The house, on the other hand, was still giving nothing away.

I maximised the window in the bottom right-hand corner. There it was, full screen. A full screen of nothing. There was something odd though. Now that I had blown it up and could see the kitchen in detail, something was niggling me. Was it the bottle of mineral water left out on the work surface? Experts have been known to rely on such intuitions: the painting in front of them is a fake; they are utterly convinced of it, even without proof. They step right back and then lean in closer, in much the same way as I was inspecting the kitchen under the magnifying glass of my fears. This tableau was a fake. The bottle had moved. While I was a) in the meeting, b) in the loo, c) on the phone or d) sidetracked by a colleague struggling to interpret a shot. Was I really, totally sure that it wasn't exactly where I had left it? For the remainder of the morning, I left my desk only to go and buy a bento box from the local Lawson, which I grazed on in front of my computer: an absence of ten minutes that I was now compensating for by not taking my eyes off the table where I would have dinner that evening. There I was, like a weatherman under house arrest in the eye of a static anticyclone. As I opened the box which held my lunch, I had the impression of looking into a doll's house from above, with all the little neatly divided compartments filled with multicoloured items of food. And I said to myself, you could fit a webcam in each of your six rooms, split the screen into the same number of windows and do nothing from morning to night but examine from a distance the bento box you live in.

And then it was lunch time. My colleagues deserted the open-plan office, the air conditioning having given up the ghost, and, preferring to swelter rather than put up with the cicadas, I went round shutting all the windows again, leaving just one open, the one on my computer screen, which I continued to watch while finishing the contents of the box compartment by compartment. Hadn't the bottle of water been slightly closer to the sink earlier on? A matter of fifteen or twenty centimetres, it seemed to me. No sooner had I convinced myself of this than I changed my mind again. You're making things up, trying to rationalise your unconscious thoughts. For that matter, are you really sure those yogurts disappeared after all? You should report it, you know, go to the police: I've had three pots of yogurt stolen in the last few months. Come on now, calm down. Lately, you've been all on edge.

That afternoon, I was talking to two new recruits who couldn't find anything better to do than pester me. While I was explaining how to use a program to design maps, I felt like banging their heads together to make them see they could not have picked a worse time to bother me. It must have been obvious from my curt tone, especially when one of them asked what the webcam at the bottom of the screen was for, *there*. I dodged the question, continuing to give explanations while all the time keeping half an eye on the kitchen. They must have thought I had OCD, or taken me for a home-loving depressive. Or was it his elderly mother's house he was watching from afar? I was about to comment on something when the rectangle in the bottom right darkened slightly. A figure was moving about on screen, shrunken (the wide-angle camera flattened everything in its field; I shouldn't have mounted it so high) and silhouetted; for a few seconds, the window that looks out onto the road was partially eclipsed. As I carried on talking to the two men next to me, I gradually realised the person I was dealing with was a woman and, judging by her hairstyle and slight frame, no longer a girl by any stretch of the imagination. She simply crossed the room and, since her head was turned the other way, I saw nothing of her face but the outline of her cheek; I couldn't make out any distinguishing features at all. Anxious not to let them sense my unease, I turned back to the two nuisances and made trivial chit-chat, trying my best to sound casual. That was a mistake. By the time I turned my attention back to her, the figure had moved out of frame. My two colleagues thanked me and left me to my empty kitchen; it was as if I had been fooled by a hallucination. She was bound to come back the other way; I just had to be patient.

Only she didn't. Ten minutes, a quarter of an hour went by. It would have been ridiculous to call the police; what exactly would I have reported? The disappearance of a shadow? I could just hear the policeman muttering as he searched the house: perhaps you're married in a parallel dimension,

Shimura-san, or maybe you thought you had at last seen the girl you would have liked to marry? (Then, leaning towards me, acting the shrink.) A girl you knew as a teenager, who turned you down just like the others? Whose arrogant features have stayed with you, lodged deep in your mind, and now that vivid memory is messing up your brain. Unless it's a fairytale elf that's moved in? We're all like you, Mr Shimura, we all have our own elves to help us through the day. Then, speaking in hushed, nudge-nudge tones and shooting me a lewd smile, he would lay out his little theory: a prostitute or a junkie, wasn't she, go on, admit it, or a girl from a massage parlour you fell for and then tired of – these things happen, we're only human – and she clung to you because she had nowhere else to go, so you decided to get her out of your hair by claiming trespass, burglary …

No! I didn't want to hear any nonsense like that. I needed proof. Police officers don't go around arresting thin air. I temporarily closed the kitchen window on my screen. My colleagues reopened those of the office and the cicadas burst in by the dozen. Filthy creatures. Behind them, the crows endlessly repeated the same *caaw, caaw* sound. And in the wings of this choir were the soloists, the bells of Urakami and the sirens of police cars chasing elves.

The cicadas were still tormenting me when I got off the tram, harpies unleashed on me, shaking their maracas in my ears. Invisibly imposing their rhythm on my walk towards insanity. I felt afraid at the thought of entering my house. From a distance, the lock did not appear to have been broken. Whether that was reassuring or not, I didn't know. Old Mrs Ota, keeping watch as always, saw me standing rooted to the pavement and called me over. She does this from time to time, motions me over and we chat about one thing or another. She once told me I reminded her of her son. Same generation, same grown-up schoolboy charm, but he has a family and lives a long way away, and only visits once a year. Or twice if I should happen to die, she joked.

Still preoccupied by the events of the afternoon, I half expected her to declare theatrically, as she does when recounting local gossip, 'I saw her coming out of your house!' But no, she only wanted to natter about this and that, and in the end it was me who asked the question. From the way she raised her eyebrows, I could see she hadn't noticed anything out of the ordinary and was almost annoyed with herself: *but I haven't moved an inch all day except to do my morning shop*. Did that mean I had dreamed the figure on my screen? Did a webcam eventually progress from scanning Formica kitchen surfaces to capturing the resident spirits, or *kami*, too? Did they record the spectres coming and going in a place thought to be empty? Over time, might the 'retina' of a camera become sensitised to what the human eye cannot perceive, the way a dog picks up ultrasound waves that his master's ears are incapable of hearing? As I made to leave, Mrs Ota threw me an oblique glance. Why do you ask? Should I have seen someone? Did you have a visitor? I assumed an air of unease, sighed softly and smiled.

'I must be becoming suspicious in my old age. There's a woman who used to clean for me, who I think kept a set of my keys. I saw her hanging around here this morning. So …'

'We're quick to suspect the worst.'

'Well, in this day and age.'

'I don't remember you having a cleaning lady, Shimura-san.'

'Oh, it wasn't for long.'

'You didn't trust her?'

I didn't reply. Without explicitly asking, I had given her reason to keep an even closer eye on things over the coming days. What deity would demand offerings of yogurt, a single pickled plum or some seaweed rice? Never mind that I was raised a Catholic, I often go to feed our *kami* at the local shrine, but it never occurred to me for one moment they would come into people's houses and help themselves.

'I think I've seen her, you know, your cleaning lady. It must have been about a month ago – I saw someone in your kitchen in the middle of the day. I said to myself, now that's odd, but then I remembered that you had a sister who comes to visit sometimes. Or perhaps he's got a girlfriend, I said to myself as well. Perhaps he's got a girlfriend.'

Her chubby face wore a look of pure kindness. Mrs Ota clearly meant well, but I dismissed her suggestion with an awkward laugh designed to hide my embarrassment.

'I thought … Time's ticking on, Mr Shimura. None of us are getting any younger! You should have a girlfriend, or you'll end up spending your old age on your own.'

After sliding the door open, I listened out for any strange noises. I had never felt this way before. Either old Mrs Ota had stopped paying attention at some point that afternoon, or the figure I had glimpsed had stolen away through a back window, sneaking out unnoticed like a ninja that just materialises and then vanishes in the same way, suddenly and soundlessly. I quickly went round inspecting the windows and noticed that one of them, in the guestroom, was unlocked. Yes, she could easily have slipped out of this room: it didn't back on to anything, no Mrs Ota on this side. Only the hills opposite, bristling with grey roofs that always make me think of a monster's scales. And this monster was falling asleep. I fastened the lock and swore to check the windows every morning before leaving the house. I felt better after closing the blinds, if still slightly on edge. I was thinking about the figure Mrs Ota had caught sight of the previous month.

As the evening wore on, my thoughts became ever more disparate. It was impossible to gather them together into one coherent whole. In the end I gave up and made myself a miserly dinner, my heart sinking as I opened the fridge. For, once again, a pot of yogurt had disappeared. I had enough information to build a picture of the intruder's dietary habits. It was grotesque. She had crossed the line. I no longer felt at home in my own house.

One by one, I opened every drawer in the living room and my bedroom. Nothing was missing; the few valuable objects I possessed were still there. Far from reassuring me, this realisation only served to heighten my anxiety. Whoever I was dealing with was *not normal*, and I felt a shiver of fear run through me. What had she come for? Once, the Queen of England had come face to face with a stranger in her bedroom at night. The guy had managed to get round all the palace security and climb in through the window to patiently await his sovereign. That was all: he just wanted a chat. Could it be that I had a fan of my own? Might hard-working nobodies like me finally be getting their own groupies?

Two days earlier I had spent my lunch hour angling for 'friends' on Facebook. I always begin my requests the same way: 'If you're from the Shimabara district too …' or 'If, like me, you live in Nagasaki …' It's like dangling a fishing rod into a whirlpool. Once I had tired of the haphazard nature of my search, which I undertake more for the thrill of it than out of genuine desire to find my soul mate (or indeed any mate), I typed in the names of a couple of truly average actors, has-beens since the earliest days of their careers. Neither had ever graduated from roles in yakuza gangster films, but both could boast groups of between three and four thousand followers. I was flabbergasted.

Enough. Everything seemed much better after two nice cold bottles of Sapporo. I no longer even felt the need to ring my sister. I put the TV on and channel-hopped before spending a few minutes watching a documentary about Hiroshi Ishiguro, the robotics professor who had developed an android in his own image. Within the next twenty years, said the voice-over, robots with human (women's!) faces will have replaced a large number of receptionists. But experts predict the greatest challenge will be overcoming the 'mysterious valley' – the unpleasant sensation when you realise there's something about the android that is not quite like us. It's not 'one of the family'. Probably in order to escape from this mysterious valley, I switched over to a live game show being beamed out of Niigata for some light relief. I didn't realise I had dozed off until an advert woke me up. QUADRUPLE-ACTION INTENSIVE ANTI-AGEING CREAM! proclaimed the beautiful redhead two metres from where I lay sprawled. Comely receptionist of the mysterious valley …

I went to lie down on the mat, but when I tried to sleep, counting off the golden rules of an ideal world as I do every night – no chance. And so it dragged on: no matter how many imaginary laws I passed, my perfectly formed society had absolutely no sedative power. When it finally came, my sleep was broken by dreams. The unconscious was bursting through. The past seeped out through hidden fault lines and names came back to me with white-hot intensity. Hizuru, Mariko or Fumiko, forgotten goddesses reappearing with a mocking laugh to say, 'We're still here. You won't get rid of us that easily.' By the time I awoke they had returned to their hiding places, leaving behind them, as they always did, a thin sheen of anxiety.

Before I left the house, I made sure the camera was working and that every exit had been secured. Although evidently the woman had had the key copied, and if she wanted to come back ... All I could do was continue the surveillance. After keeping watch all morning, I began to feel more at ease. I had checked everything carefully and tested all the locks. No one could get in. Short of walking through walls. I started to feel a little more confident. Though I still didn't leave my desk for a second, I was managing to work almost normally. No one was bothering me; no meetings had been scheduled. I had bought a bento box, a packet of salt plums and two bottles of Kirin from the Family-Mart round the corner from my house, so that I had my lunch ready to eat as soon as all my colleagues disappeared to get theirs. It was now eleven thirty and things were going well. They could have carried on like that until it was time to go home. Suddenly – having taken my eyes off the kitchen for a few seconds in order to amend the latest weather map for the Inland Sea – I caught sight of a shape, one which bore a striking resemblance to the figure I had seen the day before. Only this time, she wasn't moving. How on earth had she managed it? It was witchcraft. I couldn't make sense of it. She was standing near the window with the sunlight on her, filling up the kettle. I had her. Without a moment's hesitation, I picked up the phone and dialled the emergency services. Police? I spoke loudly and, because of that, did not notice that the entire office was listening to me. People who could never normally be torn away from their screens (why spend all that money on robots when they already exist?)

were craning their necks, raising their eyebrows and exchanging glances at the mere mention of the word 'police' in hurried, anxious tones, as if a crime had just been committed in our department and had escaped their attention until their ears pricked up. Police? This is Shimura Kobo. (I reeled off my home address.) Someone has just let themselves into my house. (I was careful not to add 'to make themselves a cup of tea'.) Right now this minute. I'm watching her – it's a woman – through a webcam. No, she doesn't seem to be armed. She's just walking around, doesn't suspect a thing … I'm at work, on the other side of town. No, I can't get there quickly, you'll have to take a master key or something for the front door – keep me updated … Yes, of course I'll come and report it. I'll be at the station in two or three hours.

I hung up. Those who had been sitting nearby crowded round me wide-eyed, almost apologetic at having overheard; they hadn't meant to, shouldn't have listened, but it was extraordinary. No doubt they were hoping I would furnish them with details to satisfy their curiosity, give them a story to tell over dinner. But they refrained from asking too many questions, showering me with sympathetic oohs and aahs I could have done without. They were all ogling the kitchen, which I had expanded on screen, and within it the woman standing sideways on, blissfully unaware of our gazes and her sudden celebrity status. And then, having gathered from my garbled commentary that I was in no state to make myself clear, they slunk away shaking their heads slightly, leaving me alone at last.

According to the clock on the computer, I had been off the phone for three minutes. And she was still there. Now that the water had reached the required temperature, she was pouring it into the teapot and steam was rising off it. She had used some of my bancha – the tea I drink in the evening because it doesn't keep me awake – taking it from the inlaid wooden box I had bought myself in Hakone the previous year. The air was much more bearable than the day before, the cicadas had turned it down a notch, and I was completely bemused by what was going on in my house. Everything appeared calm. A projection of the shared life you might have had, that was what the police officers were about to arrest, I said to myself. A reflection of your fantasies. So long as she didn't run off ... If she was making herself something to eat, she would be there for some time; long enough, in any case, for them to snare her. There she was, a doe standing in the middle of a clearing, oblivious to the fact the wolf had her in his sights. Time ticked slowly by and I continued to hold my breath. She was done for.

But then the sky cleared and sunlight poured into the kitchen. The woman stopped filling the rice cooker to look up towards the window. How sweet the morning sun felt on her skin! How bountiful it was. The stainless-steel sink glistened in the light. Her face was in three-quarter view and suddenly all I could focus on was the curved, ambered nape of her neck, the elegant throat turned by a potter's expert hands. And this neck descended sand-coloured towards a covered chest, rounded out with two small dunes. Through the glass, the woman gazed out at the miraculous sun. Eyes half shut, she let this gift from the sky flood her body; her face, which had lost its youth and frankly held little charm, luxuriated in the rays upon rays which fell upon it, launched eons ago from a star fifty million kilometres away and destined for her alone. What did it matter to her just then to be lacking in youth and charm? She was alone, or so she thought, and caught up in the joy of the moment. With her eyes still part-closed, she smiled. And I told myself she must be taking a deep breath, waving goodbye to untold fears and suffering, letting go. Maybe, just maybe, she was happy.

If she only knew! Oh! Her smile ... All of a sudden it hurt to see it. Rap on the computer screen, attract her attention ... What had I done? I grabbed the phone. At the first ring, she turned her head as though roused from a pleasant dream. Yet before long, she had returned to her previous pose. Pick up, for goodness' sake! Quick! I would have to stay on the line until she realised the call was meant for her. I kept on; nothing doing. How was she to know? How could I get my own head around the fact that, having lured her into a trap, I was now trying to get her out before it closed on her? She continued to watch the rice and let her bancha brew in spite of the ringing. Ten, eleven

... Shout at her to get the hell out before they arrive, and don't come back! Or, to put it more succinctly, they're coming to get you! Surely she would twig eventually. I glanced at my watch. The second hand was doing its rounds; time had not stood still. The woman was soaking up the rays before the next cloud appeared, and there was me wanting to scream, come on, or you won't be seeing sunlight again in a hurry!

I hung up bitterly. If you'd rather stand there and wait for the police to arrive, that's fine by me. You can even pour them tea if you like; get three or four cups out ready; you know exactly where they are. There's no more I can do. The seconds drained away, the sun vanished behind a cloud. She sorted out her rice and drank a mouthful of tea. Her eyes were wide open now and the smile that had blossomed during the sunny spell had faded. What if I tried again? She made as if to pick up, but then jumped. She stood stock still. The doe had sensed danger. And now she was stepping back, her expression changing. Stepping back, out of the camera's frame. Did she have time to make a run for it?

*

As I was to find out later when an inspector called me back, the officers had arrived at my house to find the front door locked. There were no open windows, which surprised them. After forcing the lock, they were even more flummoxed to find nobody inside. In fact the house was sealed. Believing the whole thing to be a hoax, they had been on the verge of turning round and walking out.

'We wouldn't have taken a prank like that lightly, Mr Shimura,' I was told sternly after the event. Still, just to be sure, they had searched every room. 'It was in the last room, where you keep your tatami mats, that one of our men found her, tucked away inside the oshiire with the futons.' He hadn't noticed her to begin with, because she had hoisted herself up to the top part of the closet and was huddled in the dark (he hadn't opened the doors fully). She was like a terrified animal, couldn't make the slightest sound. A curled-up little creature, that was all she was. The officer had never seen the like.

Afterwards, the inspector would ask when I intended to come in – the sooner the better – to read and sign the charge sheet. I would not hear him at first, leaving a slight gap before my reply: early this evening, I'll be as quick as I can.

For a long time after the woman had disappeared from my screen (which must have coincided with the moment they forced the lock), I couldn't stop staring at the kitchen through this mesmerising box measuring, what, ten by fifteen centimetres? It was over. In the centre of the shot, which the camera was still filming as if nothing had happened, the utensils and appliances on the work surface awaited the return of the intruder – what else could I call her? There was her cup of tea and the Zojirushi rice cooker, a white oblong like an ostrich egg or a spaceship for Lilliputians, which she had left her fingerprints on and, no doubt, a few dead skin cells. And though they were dead, those cells were teeming with atoms whose electrons were in turn twitching, along with their flocks of quarks and protons whose physical properties have hitherto eluded us but which hold the key to everything, to the universe and life. So if one day I should wish to understand the meaning of what happened in my house, I ought perhaps to collect these fossil cells now and study them.

I had to shake myself out of this daze, which mingled with my sadness – and not just any sadness. The sadness I was a major producer of, and even, as several women had told me as they were leaving me, a significant exporter. Even so I wasn't going to break down in tears at the sight of my rice cooker and, besides, a colleague had just asked me a delicate question: Well? I could have replied that the police had just entered my home and arrested a woman of a certain age preparing to eat a bowl of plain rice, but I opted for a different turn of phrase, using words like intrusion, trespass, even burglary, carefully avoiding adding that nothing was clear yet and that far from setting my mind at ease, the confusion was only increasing my anxiety.

The room they 'captured' her in is the last at the end of the corridor which runs parallel to the patch of garden between my house and my neighbour's, consisting of two bushes, two flowerbeds and a stone lantern. The room holds six tatami mats and I hardly ever go in there, keeping it for visiting relatives who generally don't visit in any case. In the bottom part of the cupboard she had chosen as her hiding place, I store nothing but futons, blankets and pillows. In the top part, nothing at all. The room itself is bare. A bedside lamp made of black wood and white paper watches over the blank space, but this beacon is almost never lit: the last visitors, my sister and her husband, came more than a year ago.

At 18.10 on this 17 July 2008, I, Terajima Masako, in my capacity as duty officer for Nagasaki district, certify that the above-named individual has attended the station to make the following statement:

'At around 11.30 this morning I was at work at Nagasaki weather station when ...'

Having read back his statement, the complainant wishes to proceed with pressing charges and has signed this declaration accordingly.

I began to read closely. A woman who had been a complete stranger to me as recently as that morning, a policewoman, had been paid to write a tiny part of my life story, and had made a very thorough job of it. She had made sense of the garbled account I had given over the phone earlier that day and put it down on paper in a logical order. A minute slice of my life perhaps, but it was one I knew would stay with me until the end. And even though I was a nobody, she had carried out her task brilliantly; I should have liked to congratulate her on it. I was touched. It was spot on. I was taking my time reading over it, mumbling aloud, but I could sense that in spite of her outward politeness she rather wished I would hurry up, so I signed on the dotted line. Afterwards, I asked her a few questions about the intruder.

'This'll surprise you, Shimura-san ... It really is an odd case ... The press are all over it already.' The press? She nodded and repeated matter-of-factly, 'The press.' Then she handed me the transcript of the woman's interview.

The above-named suspect ... admits ...

Beyond the voice of the woman who had sneaked into my house, whose words were set out on the page before me, I could hear the far-off wail of ambulance sirens, the rooks shrieking and the trilling of rush-hour trams. This'll surprise you, Shimura-san ...

My stowaway was fifty-eight, I read, two years older than me. I had thought her a bit younger when she appeared on my screen. As for her surname, it was as common as mine. She had been unemployed for a long time; so long, in fact, that she was no longer entitled to state benefits. She had once lived in a neighbourhood the other side of town, which I can't have set foot in more than two or three times. With no money coming in, she had had to give up the lease on her apartment. She couldn't bear her former neighbours to see her homeless and penniless, so she had moved on.

But what did any of this have to do with me? I looked up at the policewoman doubtfully.

'Carry on to the next page.'

She probably felt I was making a meal of it; it's true I'm not a big reader, plus I was trying to take in all the details, hoping to find some clue that would make sense of everything. In any case she decided to take over, reading aloud in her high-pitched thirty-something tones. Perhaps she felt the urge to talk down to a weatherman, confronting him with everything he had failed to forecast in his own life. She began with that well-worn opening 'one day', as though telling a fairytale:

'One day, passing your house as you're leaving, she notices you don't lock the door. She stops a little further on, pretending to wait for the tram, but she carries on watching you. It's early, you look every inch the salaryman on his way to the office. You head down the road and out of sight. It isn't very warm and it begins to rain. She umms and aahs before making her mind up. She knocks on your door; there's no reply, so she tells herself it's OK to open it. In she goes. She hovers in the hallway for a moment, on the alert. All she wants is to have a rest somewhere clean and centrally heated; she has everything she needs here.'

'But I turned the heating off in March!'

'Well, this was October. This is last autumn I'm talking about. If you'll let me finish … From your appearance, the clothes you're wearing, she guesses you'll be out at work all day. She sits down on the sofa in the living room to rest. She'll just put her feet up for a minute and then she'll be off. She feels her body relaxing. Exhausted, sleep-deprived, she nods off. She wakes up with a start. Where is she? It comes back to her. She listens out, hears nothing. What? Three hours have gone by! Never mind. She feels much better. It's midday and she can't face the thought of leaving already. It's so nice to be indoors at last, with a roof over her head ... A little while longer ... Why would she drag herself away? Where would she go? She has no family left; her last remaining links with the world are a handful of ex-colleagues she's ashamed to get in touch with, given her current circumstances. In the kitchen where you'll eventually catch her on camera, she makes herself her first cup of tea and opens the fridge.

'In the top part of the oshiire where she hid when the police arrived, the officers found an unrolled sleeping mat, a blanket, two plastic bottles, a few toiletries and a couple of items of spare clothing. I must tell you, Mr Shimura, though I'm sure you've worked it out by now, that this woman had secretly been living with you for almost a year, in this room she realised you never went in. That's right, nearly a year. Yours was not her only place of residence, mind you. There were two other addresses where she could sleep unnoticed from time to time. The first was a bungalow belonging to a travelling salesman, a bachelor who was away a lot and would mark the dates of upcoming business trips on his kitchen calendar, which she duly noted. She had also made a nest for herself in the home of a half-deaf old lady, who lived only on the ground floor of her house since she had been widowed. Having had a key cut, she could come and go as she pleased during the evenings and at night, once the old woman was asleep at the back of the house. But, as she admitted to us, it was at your house that she spent the majority of her time. Her other dens were really only back-up options in her eyes.'

Nearly a year. Suddenly I wasn't hearing anything the policewoman was saying. My head was swimming. I thought back to all those nights I had imagined myself alone, safe from the world. In my own bubble. My den, my burrow, my lair. In my turmoil I began to feel a twinge of anger building, without being quite sure who it was directed at. Everything was becoming so confused that for perhaps thirty endless seconds all external noises – the words of the policewoman, snatches of conversation among the staff, cicadas, sirens – melded into a single drone, while all I saw in front of me were bees, or rather the hollows of a honeycomb; everything had turned a greyish tone flecked with patches of light; my fingertips and toes were shaking more and more violently; I was painlessly losing control of my extremities. I felt myself gradually drifting away to some unknown place. But then I managed to draw a breath, followed by another deeper one, and little by little my unease abated. The woman speaking to me, whose voice had become oddly distant, now came back into focus. I had returned to reality.

'She had been living in your house since last autumn. And the reason she passed under the radar for so long was that her survival depended on the art of discretion. Bit by bit, however, she must have begun to feel more confident and let her guard down. As you discovered, she sometimes helped herself to food from the kitchen, thinking it would go unnoticed like everything else.

'But let me go back to the day of her arrival. She inspects the main living area. She can tell from certain unmistakable signs that you live alone. She glances this way and that before setting off down a corridor that leads to the bathroom; from there, she comes across the place where she will take up residence. That's how it all starts, she says: she opens the oshiire wide and has a good look inside. Everything in the bottom is so neatly folded. It looks as though nothing has been used for an eternity. This is a spare room, for visitors. She has a kind of epiphany: she is the person the room is for. The sun breaks through the clouds and beats on the window, which she opens a crack; it makes a warm patch on the rush mat. She sits in the shaft of light. It feels good. Bliss? Torpor, in any case, and it's in this state that time passes and ideas start coming together in her mind until they form just one: stay. A little while. The sunlight falls so sweetly on the tatami mats that she can see herself settling in here. She should just try out the closet overnight. Now she's having a shower, the first in so long. Feeling clean instantly rejuvenates her. These are her words I'm quoting. She resolves to spend a night in your home, just long enough to get her strength back. Later on, tucked away in her den, she hears you coming in …'

They handed me back the duplicate key they had found on her. I thanked them with a nod. The locks were going to be changed that evening anyway, and the key would become redundant. Darkness was falling by the time I got home. Across the bay, a string of streetlights and beacons marked the shoreline. Without turning on the light, I stood for a moment in the living room until I found the strength to open the kitchen door. Then I went in. The daylight was fading but it still etched the outlines of the teapot, the half-cup of bancha, the rice cooker and a yogurt. The police had not moved anything. And through the glass cabinet, the camera was watching me. For a second I imagined someone using it to follow my movements and picking up the phone to tell the police I was in his house. I would be caught red-handed in the kitchen and thrown into a cell. Then this man would come home and put away the things I had moved. And meanwhile, another man who believed himself to be the rightful owner of the house would have his eyes glued to the webcam and would be picking up the phone in turn.

What had actually happened was that the she-goblin who had materialised then reappeared on my screen had been caught in my trap. The objects she had abandoned that morning called to mind a photo taken out of the developing bath too soon. This still life with utensils had something of Herculaneum about it, as if caught out by the suffocating gases, and I shrank from it. By association, it somehow set me thinking about my past. All those days I had no recollection of ... Take 10 October 2006, for example. Had I done anything differently or better that day than on, say, 1 March 2003? As a meteorologist, I had a good memory for celestial events, but what did I have to show for myself down here on Earth?

And that wasn't all. The woman's presence had somehow opened a tiny window on my consciousness, and through it I was able to see a little more clearly. I understood that the year she and I had shared, even if she had avoided me and I had known nothing of her, was going to change me, and that already I was no longer quite the same. How exactly, I couldn't have said. But I knew I wouldn't escape unscathed. And looking out of the living-room bay window as the city went to sleep, I could see beyond my life, far beyond one single existence. Adjusting its focus, slowly reducing the depth of field, my gaze honed in on the wooden buildings of Dejima – the bell tower and outbuildings of the harbour's historic artificial island where, for two and a half centuries, the only foreigners to trade with the empire had been confined. Just a handful of sailors and Dutch traders in all those years. And these Europeans had never been allowed to set foot on terra firma, just a few metres away. I must have been inclined towards strange thoughts that evening, because it seemed to me that Nagasaki had for a long time remained a kind of closet right at the far end of the vast apartment that was Japan, with its four adjoining main rooms – Hokkaido, Honshu, Shikoku and Kyushu; and for all of those two hundred and fifty years, the empire had, as it were, pretended not to notice that a stowaway – that is to say, Europe – had moved into this wardrobe. And yet how many techniques, how many ideas, how much knowledge had been exchanged in both directions by way of this kind of 'false bottom'? To what extent had Dejima changed the way we saw things, during its centuries-long hibernation? As for me, I feared that the oshiire – the one in my house – and everything it had unleashed upon my feeble existence might unhinge me, leaving me vulnerable to life's open sea.

I switched on the light in the kitchen and cleaned everything from top to bottom. Then I turned up the volume on the radio, which was playing an old song about those who keep going while all around are dying. If only someone had been watching me from behind the glass cabinet and called to warn me about the pitfalls ahead; I swear I would have picked up without a moment's thought. But the telephone remained stubbornly silent. The only thing showing up on its Lilliputian screen was a missed call, the time corresponding with my attempt to alert the intruder.

Next I was standing in front of the built-in

cupboard. Two panels both two metres forty high, one sliding behind the other. The shelf was only eighty centimetres from the top. Depth? Not much more than a metre. Wood-panelled interior. A luxury couchette on a stationary train. The police officers hadn't touched anything. Futon, crumpled sheets, plastic bottles. She must only have taken her toiletries and a couple of items of clothing with her when escorted out. Under the pillow, I found a novel I had scoured the bookcase for the previous week, *Scandal*. On a page with the corner turned down, where her reading must have been interrupted, Shusaku Endo writes: 'Without warning, the cogs most central to his being had stopped turning. And the reason for it was clear. Ever since the night of …' Idiot, I said to myself, because it had just crossed my mind to send the book to her in prison to give her the chance to finish it. She must have had a good nose for these things as a matter of fact, since visitors were few and far between. My father was too old to travel. As for my sister and brother-in-law, I had been waiting for them to visit for over a year. I thought back to my stay with them at the beginning of

May; the woman must have taken the opportunity of my absence to really make herself at home. She had probably slept on the tatami mats. Was she alone in her cell tonight? I slid the panel across and backed out of the room because the doorbell had rung: the locksmith.

Later, with the television on low, I sat listening to what was going on in the world. I couldn't get interested in anything. A documentary channel was telling me all about old people and the robots who would one day make their lives easier. If I heard another word about robots ... The number of citizens of the archipelago aged 100 or older had gone from 153 in 1963 to 10,000 thirty-five years later, to 36,200 today, according to a young female journalist who was in no danger herself of joining their ranks until at least 2080. They were taking over. This year, all those celebrating their hundredth birthday were to receive a silver cup from the Prime Minister. And surprise, surprise, the silly woman had to bring Tanabe into it, hauling him in front of the cameras again just because he happened to have reached 113 ... and here's Tanabe who gets up early to read the paper, and has a glass of milk every morning. He had become our collective baby, whose crib the camera was trained on every day.

I imagined myself at a venerable age, fifty years from now. Buried deep in the mines of Brazil or the Congo lay the elements – coltan, cassiterite and other peculiar metals – that would one day be used to make my robot. This automaton would watch over the endless autumn of my days, speak to me, take down my will and hear my last breath. Someday, as it had been programmed to do, it would place a hand on my shoulder and gently whisper my name; it would pass this same hand over my eyes and mouth, dial the emergency services and set the funeral arrangements in motion. I turned off the television, plunging the house into darkness as I listened out for the sounds of the last trams, distant traffic, the on-off drone of the cicadas, the harmonious sound of the wind blowing through the bamboo, and then drops of rain as heavy as time.

*

While trying to get to sleep facing one way then the other, I couldn't shake off a persistent thought. That woman, at any point during the hundreds of nights she had spent living close to me, could have got up and stabbed me as I slept. I knew nothing about her past or her inclinations, the reasons that might have led to her putting down roots here, soiling my sheets, drying herself with my towels, crapping in my toilet, and I was furious with her. I had been completely at her mercy, and wondered if it had ever occurred to her that she could bump me off, easy as that, just because, and get away with it? I was reminded of a story by Edogawa Rampo about a man secretly living inside a sofa. Did it end with a murder? I couldn't remember and, besides, I had been living in an Edogawa novella of my own for several months and I wouldn't have wished it on anyone. The fact she had not battered me to death probably meant she had been looking for somewhere quiet, lived in and well maintained so that she could be spared too many anxieties in the senseless situation she found herself in, until a time when, perhaps, things might become clearer. She was therefore neither Madam Death nor Madam Fear. More like Madam Ordinary.

It was time I got to sleep and, lying on my back with my legs bent, I felt myself drifting off when my thoughts were hijacked again, scuppering my efforts. What if there was another woman hiding somewhere in the house? In the darkness, the absurdity of this idea made me smile, yet I began to imagine that every cupboard contained the ghost of a lost love, as though the woman caught red-handed in my house was the reflection of someone I had fallen for many years before – as a teenager, say – so long ago that I hadn't recognised her. I resolved to take one of my sleeping tablets. A mock sleep, as heavy and grey as a bloated cloud, got the better of my thoughts. It was a sleep disturbed by tortuous dreams, like a rough sea crossing at night with lightning flashing all around.

A YEAR IN HIDING

Surprised to discover that food was disappearing from his kitchen, a bachelor in his fifties from the south of the city installed a webcam which revealed that an unknown woman was roaming his house while he was out.

The owner caught the intruder in the act while watching his home from his workplace and alerted the police, believing the woman to be a burglar. Officers apprehended a woman ensconced inside an unused oshiire, where she had rolled out a mat and laid out her belongings.

'I had nowhere to live,' the unemployed 58-year-old explained. According to the police, she had been secretly sleeping there for almost a year, alternating with two other houses where she occasionally spent the night unnoticed.

I put down the copy of the *Nagasaki Shimbun*, which I never buy. The colleagues who had shown me the article had been kind and respectful. After a pause, they shook their heads as if to say, 'Well, well, the things that happen.' It's fine, I would have liked to say before I skim-read the report: something happened in my life and it's over, case closed. In reality, nothing was closed and the case was only just getting started, but I didn't want to give anything anyway. I answered their questions, playing my double role of victim and fleeting celebrity. In return, they teased me to try to cheer me up.

'You sly dog! Funny way of kicking your wife out, Shimura, offloading it onto the police!'

I smiled at the person who said this, but not too much, so as not to encourage him.

We got back to work. A typhoon had incubated far away over the China Seas, and there was a good chance it would soon be heading our way. Through force of habit, I clicked to bring my kitchen up on screen. High in the trees outside, the kites were going *kiii, kiii, kiii*. I have never really got used to their cry, any more than the way they fly. How were you to know if those *kiii, kiii* calls were hostile and meant they were about to dive-bomb you, or were merely lookout calls?

All day long my colleagues carried on gently poking fun at me until eventually I gave in and agreed to go out with them after work.

'Seeing as you're single now …'

'A few beers will do you good, Shimura.'

Once the night shift had taken over, I left with the others. Their usual haunt was a tiny establishment near the shopping arcades at Hamanomachi. Five seats at the bar, that was it, and they must have known that because there were five of us. I had never joined them there before in spite of their best efforts.

'Here we are at last!' the leader of our little group burst out, raising his glass to me with a smile that narrowed his eyes. Was he ever going to stop smiling and looking at me like that? The need to contain a burp eventually cut short his bliss.

We drank. I drink very little when I'm on my own, and since I'm on my own every day of the year ...

'Aah,' they sighed one by one. 'You're right of course, Shimura. If only we had your courage ...'

'What courage?'

'The courage to chuck our wives out!'

And we went on drinking, having lost all sense of time, in this place called Torys Bar, in conditions more cramped than a cattle truck. Two fans spluttered opposite each other, slowly turning 180 degrees in one direction and then the other as though disapprovingly shaking their heads at the amount of beer we were consuming or how much noise we were making – it could have been either. The colleagues who had dragged me to this dive were young, much younger than I, who am no longer young at all. They exchanged banter with a woman they introduced as the owner, a smiling, wrinkled lady by the name of Machiko with a scarf tied oddly around her head, giving her a pair of rabbit ears. It wasn't Machiko's fault, but her presence was making things worse. How could the others have guessed what a miserable drunk I was? Every gulp took me further away from them, while their laughter was becoming so deafeningly loud that it sometimes drowned out the music entirely.

Yukio, the most talkative member of the group, began telling a true story he had heard on the radio: on the morning of 6 August 1945, a businessman had woken up in a hotel room in Hiroshima, having arrived the previous day. The blast which devastated the city a few minutes later miraculously spared him, but he was left in a state of shock. He managed to make his way home, to Nagasaki; but two days after his return, on 9 August, the force of the second bomb threw him across his bedroom. Well, wouldn't you know it, the fellow's still going strong today, at the age of 93. And to top it off he has just been awarded substantial damages, having been the only known survivor of two atomic bombs in the space of three days.

The story met with guffaws of laughter. As for me, I found myself thinking the poor sod could use his payout to buy a multifunctional robot to look after him in his final years. Or months, as the case may be.

I went on smiling for a long time after the conclusion of the tale of the man and the two bombs (as was expected of me) and then I got up, blaming my age: can't hold my alcohol like you youngsters, it's back to work bright and early in the morning! Drawing back the *noren* curtain, I slipped out with my sadness. The Torys Bar sign carried on blinking orangey-red behind me and the last tune I heard coming from the place, a refrain familiar to all of my generation, was still going round in my head when I reached my front door. The last thing I felt like doing was going straight to bed. I could have wandered down by the river where there are a number of bars of varying repute, but I didn't have the heart for it. I didn't have the heart for anything; it had stopped.

Dismantling the camera was child's play. Deciding what to do with it afterwards, less so. Get rid of it? I could just as easily put it away in the bottom of a drawer; it wouldn't do anyone any further harm. When I had it in my hand, I found myself squeezing it tightly as if trying to crush it. Someone was behind bars thanks to this contraption! Realising I was trying to put the blame on an inanimate object, I gradually turned on myself, shouting out loud and not pulling my punches: What the hell do you want with that now? Going to put out more bait in the middle of the table and wait for another mouse to walk into the trap? Want to film the moment of capture, do you? Play it back afterwards? Do you think your kitchen's a casting room? How many lost souls do you want paraded in front of you until the right one comes along, your fairytale princess? You never managed to find her in the outside world the way everyone else does, but you think she's going to turn up here? Come on, get real, you've never even managed to hold down a relationship ...

Of course you feel better after vomiting. In what you throw up are the words that form in your brain but you never express. Rubbish along with heavy beer. I thought a shower would calm me down afterwards and I'd be overcome with tiredness. I was wrong. I lay down and waited, but it wouldn't come. Sleep? No, the ability to forget. Not that poor woman, who meant nothing to me, but my own entire existence, whose barren aridity had suddenly been revealed for all to see.

No ambition had grown from it in years, no hope either. I cursed that woman. It was because of her that the fog had lifted.

After two hours mulling over the same disappointments, I got out of bed again. I committed a crime that night: I started smoking again. Standing in the living room, with the window open to let the air in. Before long, I had had enough. I threw away the ash, angry with myself at having gone back to the filthy habit, and then I left the room. Back in the corridor, as unthinkingly as I had turned to cigarettes, I turned to the spare room.

I wanted to know what it was like. What you could hear from in there. What she might have heard of me. With some difficulty, I heaved myself up onto the top shelf. Had she once been an acrobat? A dancer? She was certainly agile. I stretched out there, in the place she had spent so many nights. My body barely fitted, my head and toes touching either end of the airless tomb. Yet I stayed there a while. These were appallingly cramped quarters, like those capsule hotel rooms, or a space capsule. How had she done it for so many nights? I lay for a long time listening to the sounds of my house and trying desperately, yes, desperately to sniff out the scent trail she might have left behind; I wanted the mattress to be steeped in the smell of her. To have taken her shape.

Outside, the past has begun to yellow. Humankind is becoming dry and brittle. When I say the past, what I mean is the time of her arrest back at the height of summer, and the evening I found myself home alone again – on my own as if a lover had dumped me. That was three months ago; it already seems so distant. I think I did my best to forget about it, and I must say the arrival of autumn has gone a long way towards making that happen. For this autumn has seeped into the soul. It has poured into us. Brought silence where there was none. At times, those walking past the dockyards do not hear the usual hammering. Gone are the echoes, clashes and cries. In the harbour, the cranes are barely loading or unloading. Elsewhere in the city where major works were in progress, the bulldozers are frozen. These dinosaurs of the industrial age have been struck down with a mysterious malady. They have spoken of it again and again on the TV, they call it the Crisis and the cure has yet to be found. The banks have stopped lending money. Some of them have no money left themselves. Where did it go? No one knows for sure, which worries everyone. An air of lethargy reigns. In the sandpit where children played at capitalism, the rules of the game have gone missing.

'Damn it, what have you done with them? You had them a minute ago!'

'What! It was you who had them just now ...'

Because the system is ailing, we are all becoming wobbly and helpless, like little children. Rumours escape from the prevailing silence like plaster crumbling from a wall. They contain words like 'restructure' and 'consultation exercise'. Even here in the weather department there's talk of cutbacks, as if there were less going on with the climate, or they could close the seas, which would be fair enough really since some of them are empty. In the space of three months, this crisis has almost made me forget that a woman bit the dust well before the rest of us and, having been homeless, is now in 'sheltered accommodation' care of the municipal prison. But now her trial is about to begin. I got my court summons yesterday. Tonight, it's not the rain that's stopping me sleeping but something else entirely – perhaps the fear of having to meet the eyes of my stowaway. Or perhaps her absence has made my life feel more incomplete than ever.

I have never liked successful people.

Not for being successful per se, but because they become defined by their success and are nothing but one big blinkered ego. Unfettered egos spell the end for all of us.

The Crisis is making everyone feel a little more alone. What do people mean when they harp on about what 'we' are going through? There is no 'we'. Instead of huddling together round a fire, all the individual 'me's are slinking off alone, eyeing one another with suspicion. Everyone thinks he's doing better than the next man, and that too probably spells the end for all of us.

Trial or no trial, crisis or no crisis, I haven't

managed to forget the stowaway. I know that according to Article 130 she is facing three years inside and a 500,000-yen fine, a fortune for a woman who probably doesn't have 10,000 to her name. Should I feel bad, and if so, about what exactly? I keep on asking myself this question, though no one else is putting it to me. My mother, when she was alive, accused me of being too sentimental. Justice must be done, she would say now, as indeed it will, but for the last few nights, yes, I've had terrible trouble sleeping.

A strange noise woke me. Something falling? Not in here – the other two are asleep and nothing has fallen over. Must have come from another cell.

Or maybe it was the rats.

I can read the time by the nightlight: almost 4 a.m. No stars in the sky, it's overcast. The only star we see in here is the spy hole. When it doesn't shine, it means a screw's watching us from the corridor. I freeze when that happens, stop thinking. Put my life on hold until the eclipse is over. The snitch … It was something similar that got me arrested, the lawyer told me. They put eyes everywhere. And there I was, going about the house without a care in the world until late afternoon … Without the camera that exposed me it would all have gone on much longer. I really liked it there. The bedroom got the sun from 1 p.m. and I used to settle down on the mats and leaf through a magazine or do nothing but top up my tan, opening the window a crack to let the air in: his tatami mats had seen better days and smelled musty. Yes, it could have gone on and on and that would have been fine by me. I always stayed on my toes, of course. When it came to my bathroom, for example, I only used it in the mornings so that everything would be dry by the time he got home. After I'd finished, I would put everything back where I had found it, just as I did in the kitchen. That meant memorising exactly where an object was before moving it out of place.

The more at home I felt there, the more wary I had to be; the temptation to let my guard down was stronger, the risk of slipping up even higher. My biggest fear was that I might shout out during a nightmare. He would have had the shock of his life hearing his cupboard scream. Having given myself away, I would have had to come up with an explanation; he would have kicked me out in the middle of the night or kept me there and called the police. To begin with, I could hardly sleep, scared stiff I was going to lose this haven where I was rebuilding myself, recovering from the bumps and bruises life had given me. Of course, I could tell myself I didn't often have nightmares. It must have been several years since I last had one and I was a long way from my past worries here. But who knows what's going to float back up to the surface? A hidden door can suddenly open in the night, letting the baddies in to take their revenge for being banished from your waking thoughts. You thought you'd seen the last of them, but they were only waiting for the clocks to strike midnight before reappearing in our night-time dramas, getting down from their Trojan horses and sowing terror around them.

In the kitchen I had to be even more attentive, to the point of obsession. Most of the time, I helped myself to food from the bins behind a local 24-hour self-service café which, by throwing out products barely past their sell-by-date, was unwittingly keeping me fed. When there was torrential rain, or if I wasn't feeling well, I drew modestly on my host's supplies, making do with rice or pasta. I took nothing he would miss. Almost nothing. Very rarely, I gave in to the temptation of a yogurt or a drop of fruit juice. That's all. With time, I had come round to his tastes; I even appreciated them.

But careful as I was, did he really notice nothing? I sometimes told myself he had found me out but was putting up with me. *And* was putting up with me. And, or but? Either way, he was working around me, the way people sometimes live alongside a mouse for a while: out of curiosity or pity. Then one day they get the traps out and the mouse is gone before you can say cheese.

In the space of a year, however, there was only one red alert. It was an afternoon in springtime, at a time of day when theoretically there should have been no need to keep an ear out. I didn't hear him come home early. The sun was so nice on the tatamis! Just right, not a ray too much. I was reading a novel I had picked at random from the bookcase in the living room. It was based on the idea of doubles and I couldn't put it down. I was lost to the world; I didn't hear the cars driving round the centre or the little Shiba yapping next door. That's when he opened the front door. The vibration of his footsteps on the floor warned me just in time. I disappeared inside the oshiire; the sliding door was open just wide enough. My leap wasn't human but an animal act, precise and soundless. A few steps more and he came into my room. I held my breath, terrified he would notice me. My final hour in this paradise had come for certain. I was wrong … A few seconds later, he put a large cardboard box down on top of the tatamis. So his coming into the room had nothing to do with me. I began to breathe again, very softly. A thin stream of air. He could have flung open the closet to put the box away inside, but he didn't. Instead, he took out a computer and various accessories.

All the time he was standing there, I only saw him in profile. His appearance up close didn't really surprise me since I had glimpsed him on the street at a distance before letting myself into his house: dull-looking, nothing special. *A decent sort.* There are hundreds of people with the same kind of nondescript face in every city. Before he had come in, I had managed to slide the door of the oshiire back across, so I was able to get a good look at him through the narrow opening without fear of being seen. There were not two metres between us. And while he stood there, I studied him intently. He was thoughtful, concentrating on the business of unpacking. It was clear he was thrilled with his gift to himself. Then he left the room. I was worried. What was he going to do with this PC? Could he be planning to connect it in here and turn the space into an office, where for all I knew he would spend the best part of his evenings surfing the web? After dinner, he returned to take everything away and set it up elsewhere, in the living room. I breathed a sweet sigh of relief. On top of that I now had a much better idea of who I was dealing with, a matter of no small importance to me. I had given human form to the footsteps, voice and cough I had overheard, and this form reassured me. He wasn't the violent sort, liable to kill me in a moment of madness or rage. And then there was the coincidence – unsettling, to say the least – that we were more or less the same age.

The next day, the way he slammed the front door and forcefully turned the key in the lock woke me with a start, as usual. But for once I didn't go back to sleep: I had an investigation to carry out. It would last for weeks and remain unfinished on the day of my arrest. Probably the most meticulous investigation ever conducted by a stranger on another stranger. I began by opening all the drawers I had been walking past without touching for months. Before long I was going through all his photos from various times in his life, some of which I recognised him in. None were labelled, so I had to rely on guesswork to establish the links between him and the people he was pictured with. Brothers, sisters, close or distant relatives, one-time lovers? Which of them did he still see, and what were his feelings for them? Which were still of this world? Everything in the house exuded an air of modesty, as it always had. I went through his payslips, those of a low-earning meteorologist. Bills informed me of his water and electricity consumption. As for phone calls, he was very sparing and never rang abroad. My investigation was stalling. I sensed an innocuous character, a simple man of the masses. I carried on regardless. Hadn't I fought for the common people, back when I was another woman?

I returned to the photos another day. As I looked

through them, I tried to establish a chronology and work out the ties that link, or linked, the people together. There was nothing attention-grabbing in Shimura's past. *Shimura Kobo*. Most likely nothing will remain of him, any more than it will of me, when he and I are gone. When I talk about myself, I have in mind my current identity, of course. The previous one has been swept under the carpet, never to be seen again, and who would be interested in that woman anyway? That's what I have in common with him, something to be neither proud nor ashamed of: being a nobody. Other than that, nothing connects us. Nobodies often differ wildly from one another. When it came down to it, there was really only one thing I wanted to find out from my fingertip search of his house, and that was when he moved in.

It's this man – not in the least attractive though by no means repulsive – who will be standing in the witness box tomorrow. I could tell the judge exactly where he hangs the suit and tie he will be wearing, the distinctive clean smell of which has stayed with me.

When I entered the courtroom he was already there, but we didn't make eye contact then or afterwards. I know he had already seen me through the lens of a video camera, but I thought he might still be curious to know what I looked like in real life. Was it a mark of supreme indifference on his part, or an expression of still-raw resentment? There was no doubt I was going to pay dearly for my stay with him. I would be handed a hefty bill for all those nights. Charged high-season rates. To be clear, I felt guilty of nothing. I was, more prosaically, embarrassed. Embarrassed to know the brand of underwear my accuser wore, his culinary and televisual tastes, what he liked to read. For I had searched everything that could be searched in this man's home, and now knew at least as much about him as his sister in Nagoya whose few letters I had read, most of them written to explain the fact that no, she wouldn't be able to come down for the holidays this time, but she would definitely visit soon. There was nothing I didn't know about his routines or obsessive tidiness, which frequently both irritated and worried me at the same time: the slightest thing out of place might prove my undoing.

Now he was calmly answering the questions put to him. I recognised the voice I had heard muffled through the sliding door of my refuge when he spoke on the phone of an evening or provided a running commentary on the NHK news for no one's benefit but his own, to the extent that I know better than anyone his tired and meek opinions and respect, bordering on deference, for the old boys' network that governs us.

Shimura did not seek to condemn me. Choosing his words carefully, he simply spelled out the situation as it was, emphasising the fact I had not stolen or broken anything in his house. Other than pinching a few things from the kitchen, which is what had eventually aroused his suspicions. Ah, so that was it! Otherwise, everything he said was to my credit. My one and only crime was having been somewhere I wasn't supposed to be. The trial must have bored him. It was boring all of us, so we did our best to get it over with as quickly as possible. Only once did Shimura's voice sound strained. It wavered slightly with emotion, and its reproachful tone came as a shock:

'I don't feel at home in my own house any more.'

I looked up at him at that point, knowing his eyes were turned towards the judge. It was the left side of his face again, as if he didn't have a right side, or kept it under wraps. He didn't look at all comfortable. He must have been desperate to get home. Perhaps he no longer felt bitter? Who could tell. I heard him say, referring to me, *the accused*, or *the woman in my house*. He never once called me by my name or pointed in my direction. The judge seemed ill at ease too, as if it was dawning on him that the case before him went beyond the generally accepted confines of decency, falling outside the bounds of the justice system, where textbook criminal law held no jurisdiction.

I got five months and no fine. 'That's a very

light sentence,' gloated my lawyer. 'You'll be out in a month since you've already served four on remand.'

I should have felt something at that stage. I knew I would eventually, but for the time being I couldn't bring myself to care about such minor victories.

It's very early on a late-autumn morning. For the past month, I have been living for this day, whose dawning I am witnessing through the barred window. Since yesterday or the day before, I have hated my cellmates less, feared them a little less. Exactly when they are going to come and fetch me, as they fetched Hiromi last month, I obviously have no idea. I'm waiting for these words: 'Pick up your stuff, you're leaving.'

Today is a Monday. Day after day, I have been hoping to be called to the visiting room. 'Visitor for you!' He must know I will soon be disappearing into the city again, maybe even moving away. I'm not the slightest bit attracted to the man and, to tell the truth, everything about the way he lives his life makes my hackles rise; but even so, I would have liked him to come and ask for an explanation. I would have liked to express my gratitude for his clemency – or was it indifference? Shimura-san, I would have begun. And then what? Perhaps I would have been so bold as to present him with the excuses that didn't come to me in court. The law has no place for excuses, and my explanations would only have made the judge smirk. It's to Shimura, and Shimura alone, I would have liked to confide all my little secrets. At the close of the trial, our eyes had met in passing for a good, slow second, and he didn't try to look away. That empty, weary gaze had well and truly fallen on me, I knew, because a shadow suddenly passed over his face; then they took me out of the courtroom.

It must be starting to feel like winter out there. It's been a bit fresh lately in the walkways. I'll end up cold when I'm free. I worry about that. It was so snug in my little nest, when our friend was none the wiser … I'm bound to feel very uncomfortable turning up in front of this Shimura, but it has to be done. Now that I have the strength to explain everything, now I've paid for my 'wrongdoing'. Is it because I was wrested from that house without warning that I'm so keen to return to it?

People are generally let out of prison in the morning, a fact she was able to ascertain for herself. It symbolises the start of a new life. You forget the what-am-I-going-to-do-and-how questions, forget the purgatory you are emerging from, and the first few hours are spent on cloud nine. They didn't amount to much, her prison wages, and she knew they wouldn't get her very far. Still, she deserved a good meal, and it was almost lunch time; she had been walking so long, she was almost drunk with walking. The restaurant windows were mouthwatering, filled with examples of the dishes on the menu. A plate of champon noodles, yes please. It had been so long … Didn't get that in prison … Satisfy your stomach and your mind's fretting will slow down.

Her first meal out since the beginning of the downturn, when she had had to give up her little furnished flat. Afterwards, she set out again. It was early afternoon. He wouldn't be getting off the tram for another three or four hours, but she had her heart set on seeing the place again on her own straight away; to renew the link with the day the police led her out in handcuffs and show herself there was continuity, or some at least. And so she made her way towards the little house she had been thrown out of and when it came into view, she smiled. She had told herself it was important to see it again. Yet a few dozen footsteps from the front door, her blood suddenly ran cold. A 'For Sale' sign was hanging outside. Before she knew it she was crashing back in time, landing with a thud as an eight-year-old when, for the very first time, she had had the terrible sensation that part of her life was being torn from her. Half a century on, the memory was still painful.

When she was eight, then, less than a year after she and her parents had moved house, her father had taken her for a walk one evening in the rainy season. It was late and humid but he was determined, and so she had gone along. They got off at a familiar tram stop in the area where they used to live. These were the pavements she had run about on with her first little playmates under the watchful eye of Mrs Kawakami. As they turned the corner, he had said, 'Look at that,' and for a long time they had both stood looking wordlessly at their former apartment block, which had been ripped wide open so that it resembled a cross-section in a geology textbook or an anatomy diagram, its rooms half devoured by bulldozers. What?! She saw the bedroom in which she had slept for the first eight years of her life as she had never seen it before: from the outside, like a tiny segment of a doll's house. One with all the furniture missing at that. Everything else was there though: the wallpapers, the doors. A sink dangled in the void. Why were her formative years being taken to pieces? Who would commit such sacrilege? That's life, her father replied, taking her into his arms, just life, and she had started to cry. I wanted to show you the house before they finish demolishing it, he whispered in her ear.

Today, the woman she had become knew better

than to leave memories knocking about in a hall of mirrors where they would go mad, like a seagull trapped inside a room. Incredulous, rooted to the pavement, she read the sorry sign once more. Then she stepped closer. She rang the doorbell, but there was no reply. A glance inside: the furniture was gone. There was a phone number on the sign which she noted down on the palm of her hand: an estate agent. A little later, the same hand pushed a coin into the slot of a pay phone. Still unbelieving, she asked if the house really was for sale and, if so, since when. Two weeks, she was told. We're holding an open house in an hour if you're interested? Caught off guard, she agreed.

What can have happened to the man? she worried to herself, sitting with the beer she had ordered. Then she remembered something. On the day of the trial, hadn't he said, rather dramatically, something along the lines of: I don't feel at home in my own house any more? So it was true … So true that he had decided to move out? Looking in the mirror in the toilets, she composed her face in a suitable expression. Soon the hour would be up: it was time to go.

*

So, after several months, here she was again inside the house, with nothing to fear this time. Just being there. It was incredible. She could have simply stayed outside and put her questions to the estate agent on the doorstep, could have said the house meant nothing to her in itself; but she crossed the threshold with the others. There were five of them, buzzing to and fro like flies on shit and asking damned stupid questions. The estate agent waited, answered. The woman lingered a while in the kitchen, then in the living room. Seeing the rooms now empty unsettled her and she feigned interest in the sale in order to hide her unease. For in its empty state, the house took her a long way back. Not a few months back, to the Shimura period, but much further into the depths of time. A thought that struck her as almost biblical crossed her mind: happy are the amnesiacs, for the past is suffering. Our creditors devoted most of their energy to snatching the possession that was our only source of riches.

Still, she was determined to complete the tour; she walked along the little corridor and went in. The others hadn't spent long in this room – rather poky and cut-off, when all was said and done – and had returned to the main part of the property. Same old tatami smell, same late-afternoon light. Her hand hesitated before sliding the cupboard door across. Same scraping of the rollers. Same shadows inside. She remained standing in front of it. Didn't hear at first when someone called her a few minutes later. It was the estate agent, standing in the doorway.

'Excuse me, madam? The visit's over now, if you wouldn't mind ... Madam?'

She caught the words 'visit' and 'over', and it made her think of the prison visiting room. She must have slipped into a trance, so he repeated himself, expressing concern at how pale she had gone.

'Is everything all right, madam?'

She shuddered and turned to face him. 'I'm coming, sorry. I was miles away.'

Then she plucked up the courage to ask her

question. The owner. Was it possible to contact him directly?

'The sale has to go via us, I'm afraid.'

'No, you misunderstand me, it's not so that I can buy it. That's not it. It's difficult to explain. I need to contact him for personal reasons. What address can I use to write to him? That's all I want to know.'

'In that case ...' The agent thought about it, and then smiled. 'In that case, send us a letter and we'll forward it, no problem.'

There is no ideal way to begin a letter to a stranger. It's true we are not total strangers, though we have only seen one another once 'in real life', and in the strangest of circumstances. I'll waste no more time on the preliminaries, Shimura-san. Above all, I wanted to express my gratitude for your restraint at the trial. That's the only word I can find for it, restraint.

She put her pen down at the end of this sentence, laying it across the paper at an angle like a fallen tree trunk blocking her train of thought. What could have felled it? A storm raging inside her skull? The woman hovered over the page, hoping to pick up where she had left off (just as staying in the same position in bed can apparently help you go back to a dream begun earlier in the night). She wanted to seal the envelope by the end of the day and pass it on to the estate agent (having added the words 'FAO Mr Shimura Kobo, the homeowner'). It would be a relief. Having waited so long for this moment, she would at last be able to explain herself. She would be able to tell herself she had recovered from her earlier shock at the 'For Sale' sign. The pad of writing paper bought before sitting down at this table struck her as dauntingly blank. How many pages must she fill? She wished there was a short cut so she could transmit her thoughts directly from her mind to his. In truth she wasn't terribly fond of writing and had hardly ever done it. And yet she must.

Restraint, or moderation if you'd rather. Either way, it meant a great deal to me, both during the trial and afterwards, when I found myself alone with my thoughts.

Please understand, this letter asks nothing of you. You have well and truly seen the back of me; I unintentionally hurt you and will not do so again. Only, when

I saw the 'For Sale' sign at your door, my elation at having regained my freedom turned to sadness, and I selfishly said to myself: we're on the same footing now, he and I, both banished from the same kingdom. Please forgive me for having had such a shameful thought, which I quickly dismissed but wanted to share with you all the same. I would also like to ask your forgiveness for all the trouble I've caused you; what you said at the trial has stuck in my mind: I can't live there any more.

No doubt you will be wondering why I am poking my nose in, having been the cause of all this, and how exactly I can claim to have an attachment to something that was not mine but belonged to you. This will surprise you, but the truth is that, despite appearances, my attachment to that house was actually deeper than yours, and the reason I am writing is to explain how my moving into your house had nothing to do with chance, contrary to the impression given by the investigation.

As you heard during the trial, I found myself out of work two years ago. At my age, I had no prospect of finding another job. Retirement was still a long way off, but I no longer had a place in the world of work. I was condemned to be neither one thing nor the other. Cursed are the single and childless! Once I was no longer entitled to unemployment benefit, I had to give up my lease. The first stirrings of shame drove me out of my neighbourhood.

After selling the handful of electronic devices and decorative trinkets that I had about me, I realised that everything that mattered to me could easily fit inside a small rucksack and a shopping trolley. I found myself on the streets in high summer, last year. The rainy season had come to an end a good week earlier. It was the ideal time to learn to sleep outdoors, and learn I did. At night, I settled down a few metres beyond the last houses on the hill, which often lay empty and were insalubrious - but I imagine you know the top part of town as well as I do - surrounded by cemeteries and temples harking back to bygone days, and I was not to be pitied. At that time of year, everything still seems easy. But I won't go into the whole story of those strange few weeks which count, if not among the happiest, then at least among the freest of my life. I went out walking in the cooler hours in search of food; when it was too humid, I simply floated above the city in the perfect shade of the bamboos.

What did I have left? At night, lying down, the same thought kept coming back to me: this whole thing is a prank. One big joke. Sooner or later, I'll get an explanation. I'll be offered excuses and I will know the truth. We will all achieve enlightenment. It's destined to happen, only we don't know when. You just have to be patient. And when the time comes, we'll escape this absurd drama. The trail of breadcrumbs leads towards the emergency exit.

But the time didn't come. Every night, I lay down full of confidence. It was all a bit of fun and everything would be back to normal in the morning ... It simply wasn't possible that everything could be so utterly senseless, the stars, the wind, humankind.

If there's one thing I became sure of in the course of those weeks, it was this: there is no meaning. That is to say, it didn't exist before we did. The idea of meaning was invented by humans as a balm to their anxieties, and their quest to find it is obsessive, all-consuming. But there is no Great Architect looking down on us from on high. Sometimes, when this realisation made my head spin, I needed a lifeline; I would spread my things out in front of me, keepsakes I had not been able to part with. It was not that I expected them to save me. Yet a pale, cold light radiated from them, like a foundation for the universe; this light had something of the brightness of the stars, for the faces which appeared in my photos were most often those of people who had passed away; the factories where my few cherished possessions had been manufactured must have long ago closed their doors; as for the old key that had never left my side, it had been without a door to open since time immemorial.

Autumn was approaching. The early hours were cooler. Twice I had been caught in the rain as I slept and had been driven from my bamboo. Drenched, I had taken refuge in an abandoned shack a little way down the hill, and waited for the sky to plug its leaks. I couldn't make the quiet life I had been leading last much longer, and the knowledge worried me, even panicked me at times. It didn't cross my mind for one moment that I might move into one of those hovels permanently; they disgusted me. From then on, I began to wander about in search of shelter. Anyone with time to watch the goings-on of a street soon works out who lives alone and what their habits are. For example, some elderly people leave their doors unlocked when they go out shopping. I 'inspected' several somewhat isolated houses down overgrown cul-de-sacs. To begin with, I only sheltered in them on nights when it rained heavily. A storm trapped me inside the home of a deaf woman for forty-eight hours. During the day, when the downpours were more spaced out, I continued my walks; in the course of my wandering, I sometimes ended up in the neighbourhood where I had spent my happiest years: between the ages of eight and sixteen. Oh what precious years they were! I kept a lookout for several mornings in a row. Some distance away, I saw a man leaving at around eight o'clock every morning from the house in which I had grown up. In all likelihood he was on his way to work somewhere. Maybe ... I was seized with the desire to see it again. The entrance to your house was really only overlooked by the property opposite. One morning, I was lucky and the old lady who lived there decided to leave the house. She walked slowly down the road, which was otherwise empty. Maybe ... I thought I'd give it a go, walked a few paces and rang the bell. There was no one in. You lived well and truly alone. In spite of all the years that had passed, the locks had not been changed. And in any case, you had neglected to lock up that day. There was no need to put my key to use. Before I knew it, I was stepping inside the old kingdom. That is how I found myself in your home one early autumn day, Shimura-san.

It is said that certain breeds of sea turtle come back to die on the beaches where they were born. It is said that salmon leave the sea and come upstream to spawn in the rivers where they grew up. Life is governed by such protocols. Having completed a sizeable cycle of my existence, I was returning to one of my oldest habitats. Site of my eight-year-long 'age of discovery'. An age of wonder and untold promise. I dare say in recent times you rarely stopped to appreciate the view from the window of what had been my bedroom – and became yours, many years later. You had perhaps become blasé about it. But imagine what it meant for a little girl like me to take in the sight of Mount Inasa and the bay, the dockyards and all the boats, all at once. Leaning a little to the left, I could see Oura church where I had been baptised, or all the way over to the right, the distant northern neighbourhoods; strange, these Catholic areas razed to the ground by a Christian country's bomb ... There are so few Christians in Japan, it's as if the raging atoms dumped by America had meant to play a tasteless trick on them.

I loved my bedroom, my balcony on the world, a world reborn after the deaths of many of my ancestors, one 9 August long ago. Eight of my years went by there. How I loved those rooms, those walls ... It seems to me it should be written into the constitution of every country that every person should have the inalienable right to return to the significant places of their past, at a time of their choosing. They should be handed a bunch of keys giving them access to all the flats, houses and gardens in which their childhood was played out, and allowed to spend whole hours in these winter palaces of the memory. Never must the new owners be allowed to stand in the way of these pilgrims of time. I believe this strongly, and should I become politically engaged again, I think it would be the sole focus of my manifesto, my one and only campaign pledge.

One Sunday in autumn, the year I turned sixteen, my parents drove to near Shimabara to visit some cousins. They never came back. A landslide caused by the storm we were having swept the road away beneath them, somewhere up in the mountains. And that was that. I was an orphan. My remaining family members took me in. I went to live with an uncle and aunt. I remember the day I moved out. I never dreamed I would one day come crawling back like a petty thief to hole up in the room my parents had once slept in.

Later, I managed to get into university, in Fukuoka. My studies did not go well. I couldn't stick at anything. Little by little, I came to see that the landslide was still going on inside me. It had taken its first prey one day in the typhoon; now it was my turn. The ground continued to crumble, only more slowly and insidiously this time. Piece by piece, it took apart the life I would have liked to lead. Whatever I did, everything fell from my grasp. Some part of the mechanism must have broken. I began to hate the way the world was going and got in with a certain crowd. In 1970, at the age of twenty, I joined the highly subversive United Red Army. The renewal of the security treaty between our country and the United States continued to ally us with the people who had dropped an atomic bomb on my family. The hatred I felt! I spent years hating. Everything else was beside the point. I devoted myself to my red dreams the way others devote themselves to oil painting. But I couldn't even take my taste for the extreme seriously. We had a passion for failure while hurling victory slogans. One day, some of the group were arrested. I had to lie low. I ended up getting into drugs and my former self dissolved, the self I had been trying to escape by becoming part of a collective movement. I was given a new identity, brand-new papers. I had a succession of salaried jobs and was never able to seize the second chance that my new name offered me. That's all there is.

February 2009–April 2010